For Merryn and
magical Auntie Floh
A S

For Iris B
N E

EGMONT
We bring stories to life

First published in Great Britain 2017 by Egmont UK Limited,
The Yellow Building, 1 Nicholas Road, London W11 4AN
www.egmont.co.uk

Text copyright © Amy Sparkes 2017
Illustrations copyright © Nick East 2017

Amy Sparkes and Nick East have asserted their moral rights.

ISBN 978 1 4052 7379 4

A CIP catalogue record for this title is available from the British Library.

Stay safe online. Egmont is not responsible for content hosted by third parties.

Amy Sparkes is donating 5% of her author royalties to ICP Support,
aiming for every ICP baby to be born safely Reg. charity no. 1146449 www.

Ellie's Magic Wellies

By Amy Sparkes

Illustrated by Nick East

One miserable day it rained and it poured.

Ellie Pengelly was fed up and bored.

Until at the door came a rat-a-tat-tat!

And there stood Aunt Flo with her marvellous hat!

"I'm late for the dentist," said Mum. "I must go!
But you stay and play with your dear Auntie Flo."

GIVE IT WELLIE

Her aunt gave a smile,

"You won't be bored, Ellie.
I've brought you a pair of . . .

fantabulous
wellies!"

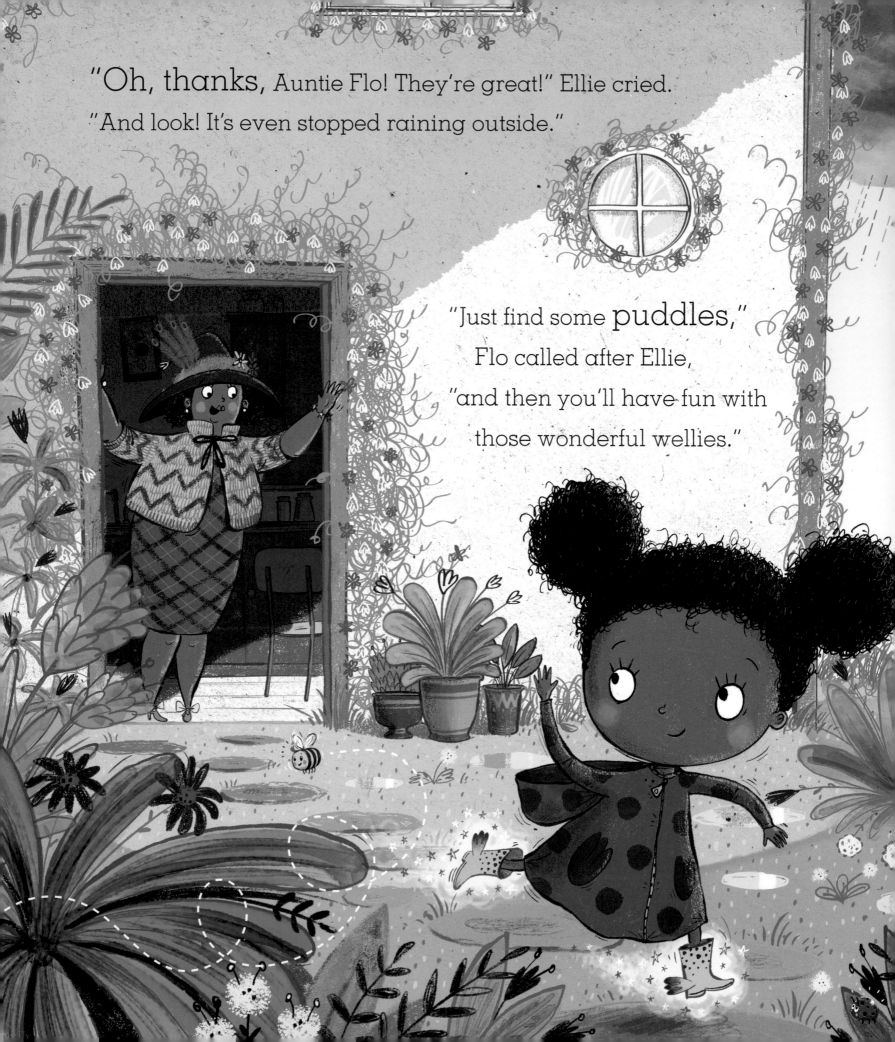

"Oh, thanks, Auntie Flo! They're great!" Ellie cried.
"And look! It's even stopped raining outside."

"Just find some puddles,"
Flo called after Ellie,
"and then you'll have fun with
those wonderful wellies."

Ellie found a **big puddle** for splashing about,

but as she

j
u
m
p
e
d

in . . .

. . . a strange creature

jumped out!

SPLISH
SPLASH

SPLOSH!

"My wellies are **magic**!"
cried Ellie with glee.

The creature bowed low
as he said happily,

"I'm a
Flibberty-Gibberty,
hip, hip, hooray!
I'm out of my puddle
and ready to play!

Let's **wriggle!** Let's **giggle!** Let's skip to the sky.

Play **hippity-hopscotch** and flap till we fly.

Let's **zippedy-zoom.** That's just what I like!"
The Flibberty said as he hopped on the bike.

But after a while, Ellie ran out of puff.

"I'm tired," she said.
"Haven't YOU had enough?"

"Nonsense
and flip-flap," the Flibberty said.
"No time for flop-flopping!
Come, stand on your head!"

A thought came to Ellie,
"Let's go in and eat."

The Flibberty clapped.
"A *splendiddly* treat."

He darted inside . . .

. . . flinging open the door,
and **emptied** the fridge
out on Mum's kitchen floor!

"Let's **juggle** with jam
and **jiggle** with jelly!

Let's guzzle and gobble," he giggled to Ellie.

She looked at the floor. "We should tidy away . . ."

But Flibberty said,
"Why, there's still time to play . . .

Let's zoom through the rooms,

bounce-a-bounce

on the beds.

Let's **flubble** with bubbles . . .

and wear **pants** on our head!"

Then Auntie Flo called,

"That was Mum on the phone.

She rang up to say that she's on her way home."

"Home?" squeaked Ellie. "But look at this mess!
Oh, put down that lipstick and take off that dress!

We've both turned the house upside-down everywhere,
but I'll be in trouble – that just isn't fair."

The Flibberty blushed.

"From my tail to my paws,

I'm most muchly sorry

for trouble I cause."

Ellie couldn't stay cross, as she watched her friend bow,

but she needed a plan and she needed it now.

"I know," said Ellie, "now listen to me.
If we tidy together, how fast could we be?"

The Flibberty clapped, "We'll be quick as a flick.
And tidy in half of a tickety-tick!"

WHOOSH

The magical wellies made Ellie's feet zoom
and soon they had straightened up all of the rooms.

Then they ran to the garden and found Flibberty's puddle.
"I'm glad you could play!" Ellie gave him a cuddle.

"So fabbity funderful!"
her new friend said.

"But now I am ready for snoozles in bed."

They held hands and
jumped with a **fabulous**

S P L A
S
H!

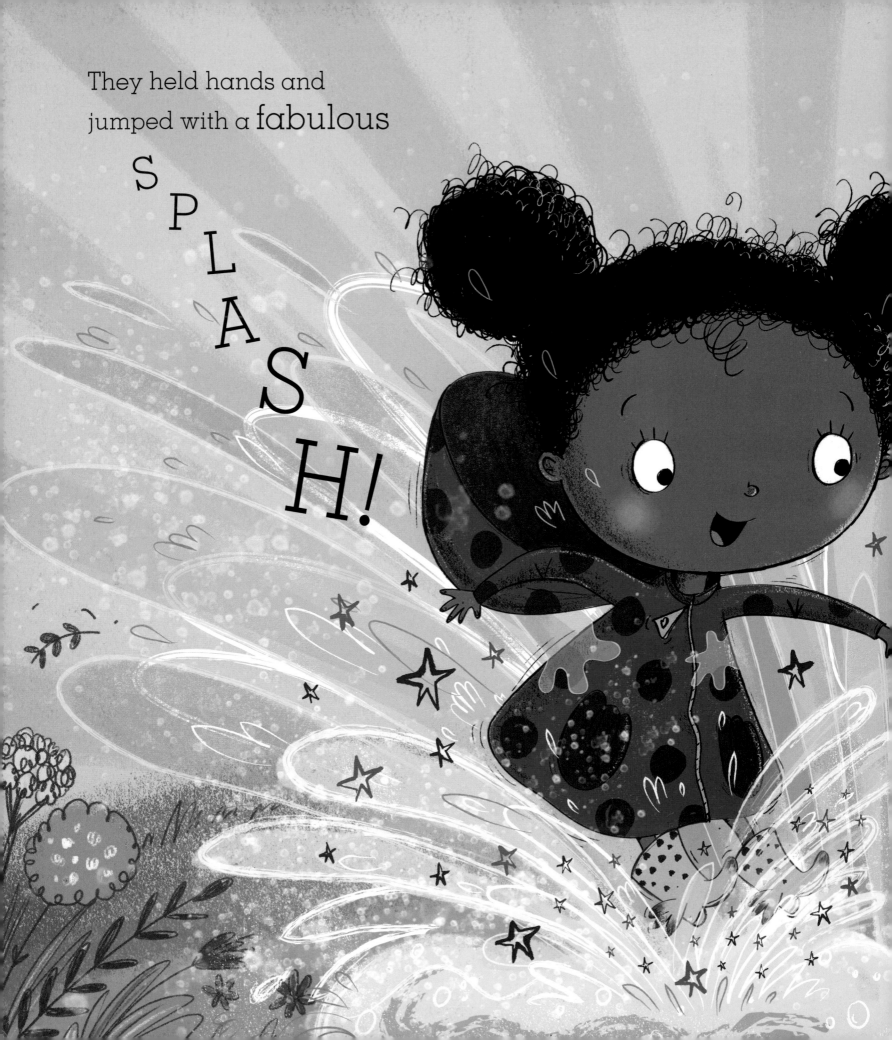

And *Flibberty* vanished as quick as a flash.

Just then Mum appeared with Aunt Flo at her side.

"Nice wellies!" said Mum. "Are you coming inside?"

"Oh no!" Ellie said. "I would **much** rather stay and play in our puddly garden all day!"

"Now I'm off for another adventure," said Ellie,

"More fantabulous fun with my . . .

magical
wellies!"

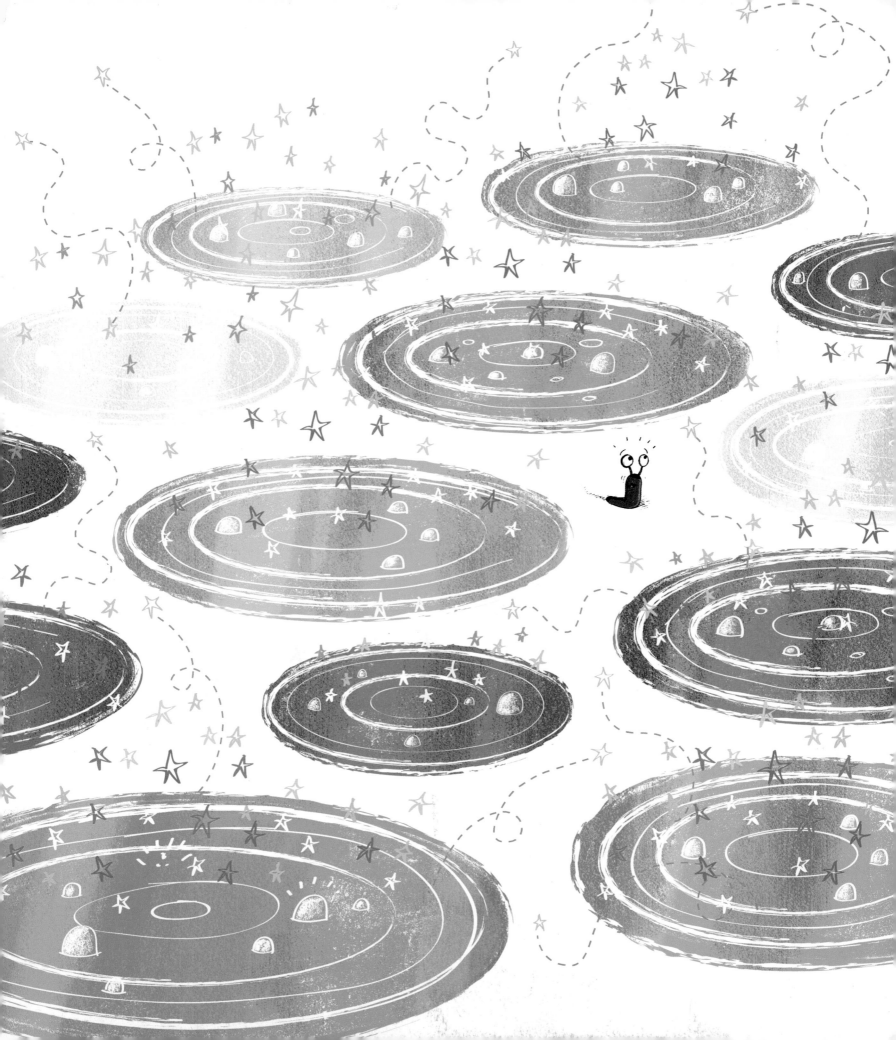